RETOLD BY
AUBREY DAVIS
SODY SALLERATUS

ILLUSTRATED BY
ALAN AND LEA DANIEL

Kids Can Press

To Richard Chase, and to the students of
the Metropolitan Toronto School Board,
who taught me how to tell this tale —
A.D.

To Ethan, Kieran and Joe —
A. and L.D.

First U.S. edition 1998

Kids Can Press Ltd. acknowledges with appreciation the assistance of the Canada Council
and the Ontario Arts Council in the production of this book.

Published in Canada by
Kids Can Press Ltd.
29 Birch Avenue
Toronto, ON M4V 1E2

Published in U.S. by
Kids Can Press Ltd.
85 River Rock Drive, Suite 202
Buffalo, NY 14207

The artwork in this book was rendered in pencil and acrylic on Arches watercolor paper.
Text is set in Palatino.

Edited by Charis Wahl and Debbie Rogosin
Printed in Hong Kong by Wing King Tong Company Limited

CMC 96 0 9 8 7 6 5 4 3 2

Canadian Cataloguing in Publication Data

Davis, Aubrey
Sody salleratus

ISBN 1-55074-281-7

1. Picture books for children. I. Daniel, Alan, 1939 — II. Daniel, Lea. III. Title.
PS8557.A832S63 1996   jC813'.54   C95-933081-X   PZ7.D38So 1996

Saleratus (pronounced *sa-le-ray-dus*) is a 19th-century American word for baking soda. In Latin, saleratus means aerated salt — a reference to baking soda's leavening properties.

Once upon a time there was an old
woman, an old man, a girl, a boy and a
squirrel that lived on the mantelpiece.

One day the old woman wanted to bake
biscuits but she had no baking soda.

"Go buy me some Sody Salleratus," she
said to the boy.

So off he went down the road.
A-HIPPITY-HOP.
HIPPITY-HOP.
HIPPITY-HOP.

Over the bridge.
HUMPITY-HUMP.
HUMPITY-HUMP.
Down to the store.

"Hey, Mr. Grocer," said the boy. "May I have some Sody Salleratus, please?"

"Baking soda is what you want," replied the grocer. He gave the boy a boxful.

The boy paid him a nickel and
headed back home.
A-HIPPITY-HOP.
HIPPITY-HOP.
HIPPITY-HOP.
Over the bridge.
HUMPITY-HUMP.
HUMPITY-HUMP.

Now, under the bridge there lived
a hairy, smelly bear.
"GRRR!" growled the bear.
"Who's that walking on my bridge?"
"It's me — Boy. Me and my Sody
Salleratus."

"RAWR!" roared the bear. "I'm going to eat you and your Sody Salleratus!"

And he did.

The old woman, the old man, the girl and the squirrel waited and waited.

Finally, the old woman said, "Girl, go down the road and find Boy."

So off she went down the road.

A-Skippity-Skip.

Skippity-Skip.

Skippity-Skip.

Over the bridge.

Skumpity-Skump.

Skumpity-Skump.

"GRRR!" growled the bear. "Who's that walking on my bridge?"

"It's me — Girl."

"RAWR!" roared the bear.
"I ate Boy and his Sody Salleratus. And
now I'm going to eat *you*!"

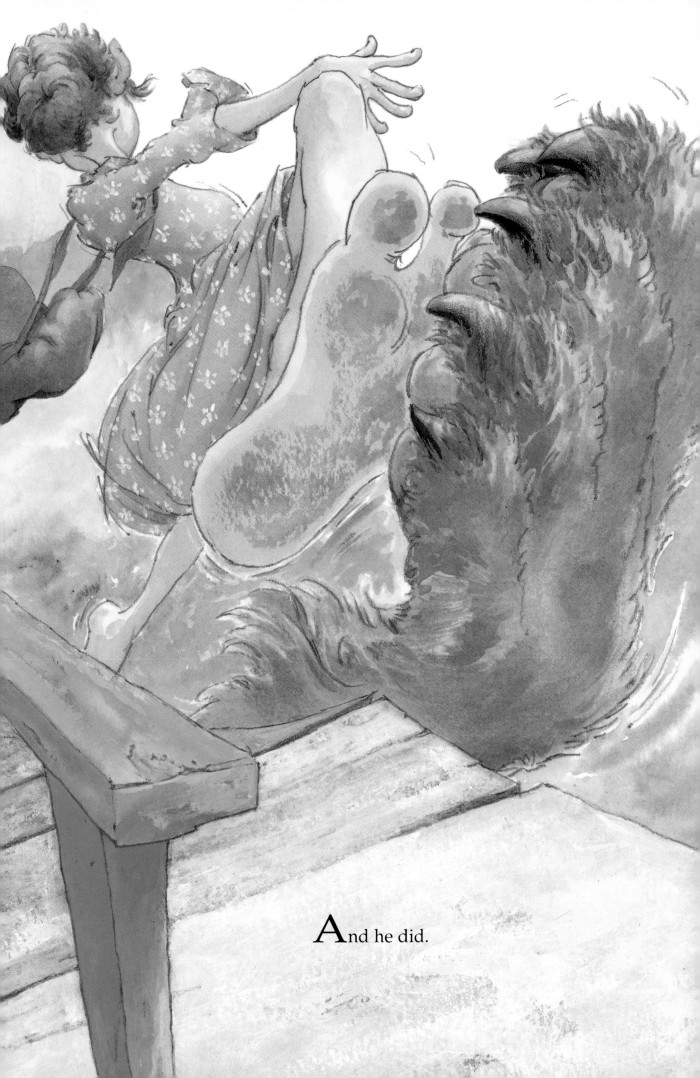

And he did.

The old woman, the old man and the squirrel waited and waited.

Finally, the old woman said, "Old Man, go down the road and find Boy and Girl."

So off he went down the road.
A-CRICKITY-CRACK.
CRICKITY-CRACK.
CRICKITY-CRACK.

Over the bridge.
CRUNKITY-CRUNK.
CRUNKITY-CRUNK.
"GRRR!" growled the bear. "Who's
that walking on my bridge?"
"It's me — Old Man."

"RAWR!" roared the bear.
"I ate Girl. I ate Boy and his Sody Salleratus.
And now I'm going to eat *you*!"

And he did.

The old woman and the squirrel waited and waited.

Finally the old woman said, "I'll find Boy and Girl — and Old Man, too."

So off she went down the road.

A-Limpity-Limp.

Limpity-Limp.

Limpity-Limp.

Over the bridge.

Lumpity-Lump.

Lumpity-Lump.

"GRRR!" growled the bear. "Who's that walking on my bridge?"

"It's me — Old Woman."

"RAWR!" roared the bear.
"I ate Old Man. I ate Girl. I ate Boy and his
Sody Salleratus. And now I'm going to eat *you*!"

And he did.

The squirrel waited on the mantelpiece, all by himself. He waited and waited and waited.

Finally, the squirrel said, "I'll find Boy and Girl and Old Man — and Old Woman, too."

So off he went down the road.

A-CHIPPITY-CHIP.

CHIPPITY-CHIP.

CHIPPITY-CHIP.

Over the bridge.

CHUMPITY-CHUMP.

CHUMPITY-CHUMP.

"GRRR!" growled the bear. "Who's that walking on my bridge?"

"It's me — Squirrel."

"RAWR!" roared the
bear. "I ate Old Woman. I ate Old
Man. I ate Girl. I ate Boy and his
Sody Salleratus. And now I'm going
to eat *you!*"

But the squirrel ran to a tree and
climbed up and up and up.

The bear climbed up and up
the tree, too.

The squirrel climbed higher and higher and higher.

The bear climbed higher, too.

The squirrel ran onto a branch.

The bear ran onto the branch, too.

The squirrel bounced on the end of the branch.

A-Boing.

A-Boing.

A-Boing.

Then he jumped to another tree.

The bear bounced on the end
of the branch, too.
A-Bong.
A-Bong.
A — CRACK!

The branch broke.
Down fell the bear.
Down
and
down
and
down.

BOOM!

The bear busted wide open.
Out stepped the old woman.
Out stepped the old man.
Out stepped the girl.
Out stepped the boy.
"Boy," said the old woman.
"Where's my Sody Salleratus?"
"Here," he said. And they all
went home.

That night the old woman baked a heap of biscuits with that Sody Salleratus. Everyone ate and ate and ate.

And guess who ate the most of all.